The Horse and Pony Quiz Book

Sandy Ransford

ISBN: 978-1-934983-69-0

Stabenfeldt, Inc.
225 Park Avenue South
New York, NY 10003
www.pony.us

Available exclusively through PONY.

Contents

Contents

Introduction

How much do you know about the world of horses and ponies? Here's your chance to find out! There are quizzes and puzzles on all aspects of riding and pony care, with questions on breeds and colors, tack and trimming, conformation and competitions, stabling and feeding, schooling and jumping, and much, much more. There are teasers to baffle your brain, and picture puzzles that are fun as well as perplexing. If you get stuck, the answers are at the back, but don't give up too quickly!

Happy puzzling!

Quizzes

Ponies! Ponies! Ponies!

Here is a group of ponies grazing happily in their field. Each pony has its name by its side – but have they been given the correct names? Read what we know about them in the list before you answer.

biscuit

Silver

Snowball

Bella

Biscuit

Silver

Snowball

√ Silver is a dapple gray.
√ Bella is a bright chestnut.
√ Rhoda is a bay, and has her foal by her side.
√ Jewel is a liver chestnut.
√ Snowball is a gray, but is almost white all over.
√ Jess is a dark bay, and also has a foal with her.
√ Biscuit is a yellow dun with black points.
√ Daisy is a dark bay with three white socks.

Make and Shape

1. Which two parts of a pony's limbs should be sloping?

2. What is a ewe neck?

3. What is a dished face, and what breed of horse is famous for it?

4. What do people mean when they say a horse has 8 inches (20 cm) of bone?

5. What are hocks that turn inwards like this called?

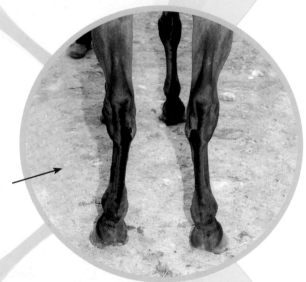

6. Which of the pony's legs carry more weight – the front or the back?

7. What are lop ears?

8. Where on a pony is the coronary band?

9. What are feet that turn inwards at the toes, like this, called?

10. Is it better for a pony to have a broad chest or a narrow one?

11. What is a goose rump?

12. What is a back shaped like this called?

13. When seen from the front, should a pony's knees be flat or rounded?

14. Which part of a horse or pony is its "engine," i.e. the part that drives it forwards?

Why?

1. Why do people often tie a pony's lead-rope to a loop of string rather than directly to a tying-ring?

2. Why is it important to clean your tack regularly?

3. Why do show ponies and horses often have braided manes?

4. Why do some riders use rubber-covered reins?

5. Why do we feed hay in a hay net, and what must you consider when doing so?

6. Why do we mount horses and ponies from their left sides?

7. Why is it important that a stable has good ventilation?

8. Why do some curb bits have a lip strap?

Name the Markings

Do you know the names of these leg markings?

1.

2.

3.

4.

5.

6.

7. hoof

13

Mounting and Dismounting

1. Before you put your foot in the stirrup, which way do you turn the stirrup iron?

2. Which foot do you put in the stirrup? *Left*

3. How can you prevent a pony from walking forwards when you mount it? *grabing the reins before getitng on*

4. As you swing your leg over the pony's back, what must you be careful not to do?
Slam your Leg down

5. Has this stirrup iron been turned the correct way for the right foot? *No*

6. What is this way of mounting called?

7. What is this and why would you use it?

[handwritten: mounting block]

[handwritten: to get on]

8. If you always mount from the same side, what should you do with your stirrup leathers?

9. What's the first thing you do when dismounting?

[handwritten: Drop your styrups]

10. In which hand do you hold the reins as you dismount?

[handwritten: left]

11. As you are dismounting, what do you do with your upper body?

12. As you land on the ground, what do you do with the reins?

[handwritten: Put them over the Rons Head]

[handwritten: Bring them over the horses head]

15

Baffling Brainteasers

Here are some fiendish puzzles to test your brainpower!

1. Over a number of years a mare had several foals. Her last foal, a filly named Sunset, had as many sisters as she had brothers, but each of her brothers had twice as many sisters as he had brothers. How many filly foals and how many colt foals did the mare have?

2. Mrs. Brown and Mrs. Black were driving their children and their ponies to two different horse shows. Mrs. Brown drove from Alphaville to Betaville, which is 185 miles, at an average speed of 50 mph. Mrs. Black drove from Benton to Dunton, which is 115 miles, at an average speed of 35 mph. If they both set out at 9 a.m., who arrived at their destination first?

3. Susie went out into the orchard to collect fallen apples for the ponies. When she'd filled her bag she went to the stables and gave half of the apples to Jason and Jasper, one-fifth of the remainder to Sorrel, and a quarter of what remained after that to Betsy, leaving her three apples each for Cleo and Freddie. How many apples did Susie have in the bag to start with?

4. Ella had a 10-year-old skewbald mare, the same age as she. When she asked her father how old he was, he replied, "Your age is now a quarter of mine, but five years ago it was only one-seventh." How old is Ella's father?

5. Jill and George are brother and sister, and they each own a palomino pony. Jill's pony is eight years old. If George's pony is half as old as Jill's, how many years ago was it twice as old as hers was?

Odd One Out

These pictures of a pony enjoying a roll in the field may all look identical, but one of them is different. Can you spot which one it is?

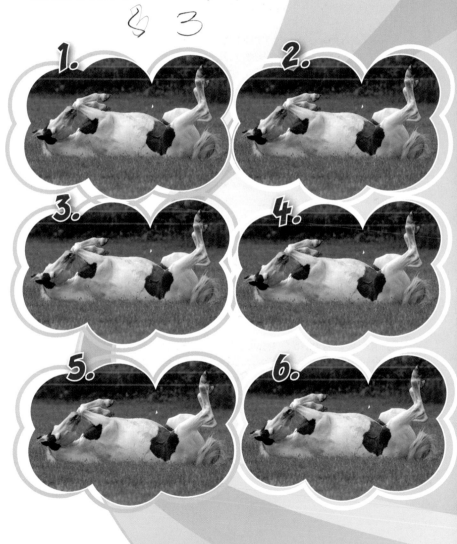

Walk On

You're sitting in the saddle, but what comes next? See how much you know about the basic aids. You have a one in three chance of getting each answer right.

(N.B. A half-halt is a preparatory aid before changing pace or direction. The rider gets the horse's attention by increasing contact with the lower legs and slightly increases the rein contact to contain the energy created.)

1. What does the word "aids" mean? Does it mean ...
a) Parts of the saddle that help you sit comfortably on the pony, such as stirrups?
b) The signals a rider gives a pony to tell it what he or she wants it to do?
c) Parts of the pony's tack other than the saddle and bridle, such as martingales?

2. What signals do you give a pony to tell it to walk on? Do you ...
a) Squeeze with the calves of your legs and relax the pressure on the reins a little?
b) Kick with your heels and let the reins go loose?
c) Flap your legs against the saddle and shake the reins?

3. You're walking along and you want to turn right. Do you ...

a) Look to the right. Do a half-halt. Take a light contact with the rein in your right hand, press with your left leg behind the girth and with your right leg on the girth?
b) Bring the left rein across the pony's neck and press with your right leg behind the girth?
c) Pull on the right rein and press with both legs behind the girth?

4. How do you stop the pony? Do you ...
a) Pull on the reins with both hands and take your legs away from the pony's sides?
b) Press your legs into the pony's sides and let the reins go loose?
c) Do a half-halt. Sit deep in the saddle, press both legs into the pony's sides and resist its forward movement by holding the reins firmly?

18

5. If you are walking on a loose rein and you want to trot, what do you do? Do you ...

a) Shorten your reins and squeeze the pony behind the girth with both legs?

b) Lengthen your reins and squeeze the pony behind the girth with both legs?

c) Pull on your reins and kick the pony with your heels?

6. If you are cantering and you lean forward, what will the pony think you want it to do? Is it ...

a) To go faster?

b) To slow down?

c) To maintain the same pace?

7. How do you get a pony to canter with the right leg leading? Do you ...

a) Do a half-halt. Squeeze with both legs behind the girth and feel your right rein?

b) Do a half-halt. Squeeze with your right leg behind the girth, keep your left leg pressed on the girth and feel your left rein?

c) Do a half-halt. Squeeze with your left leg behind the girth, keep your right leg pressed on the girth and feel your right rein?

Saddling Up

1. Does a saddle rest on the pony's spine?

2. Where does a saddle sit in relation to the pony's withers?

3. From which side of the pony do you put on a saddle?

Left

4. What is the function of the "girth safes" – the small pieces of leather that slide onto the girth straps?

5. How do you fasten the girth on a horse that dislikes it?

6. What do you call the saddle-shaped pad that fits under the saddle?

7. How is this pad attached to the saddle?

8. What's the best way to store a saddle?

9. What is the framework on which a saddle is constructed called?

Tree

10. How many fingers should you be able to fit between the pommel of the saddle and the pony?

Parts of the Saddle

Can you name the numbered parts of the saddle?

Panel
1

Seat
2

Cournet
3

4

5

6
strup leather

7 sturp

8

girth

9

True or False?

How many of these statements are true, and how many are false?

1. The American Quarter Horse got its name because it was originally bred to race over a quarter of a mile (402 meters).

true

2. Palomino horses are black and white.

false

3. A livery yard is a place where packs of hounds are kept.

false

4. This rider's foot is in the correct position.

false

5. Wood shavings make good bedding material for horses and ponies.

True

6. Horses and ponies with blue (wall) eyes have poor eyesight.

True

7. This growth, on a horse's leg, is called a chestnut.

true

8. A pony's front feet are a different shape from their hind feet.

False

9. This kind of comb is used to clean a body brush.

False

10. Feeding a lot of oats is very good for a pony.

False

11. Ragwort is a poisonous plant which must be removed from a pony's field.

True

12. A shoe with a groove in it, like this, is called a fullered shoe.

False

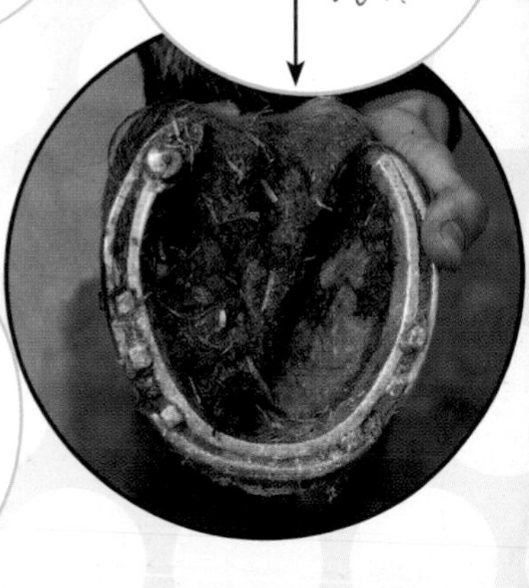

13. "Changing the rein" means riding in the opposite direction around the ring.

14. A "flying change" means going in the opposite direction at great speed.

False

23

What's Wrong?

This stable yard is a lesson in how not to do things! There are an awful lot of deliberate mistakes here. How many can you spot?

25

A Pony's Paces

1. What are a pony's four natural paces?

Walk, Trot, Canter, Gallop

2. How does a pony move its legs when trotting?

3. How does a pony move its legs when pacing?

4. Is there a moment in canter and gallop when all the pony's feet are off the ground at the same time?

5. What is a pony's fastest pace?

6. What is the tölt?

7. Which breed of pony is most famous for performing the tölt?

8. How many beats to the stride are there in canter?

9. What is the difference between working canter and collected canter?

10. What happens to a pony's head and neck positions when it is carrying out a free walk on a long rein?

Galloping Ponies

There are an awful lot of ponies in this picture! Something has spooked them, so they are charging around in all directions. How many ponies are galloping to the left, and how many are galloping to the right?

Good Grooming

1. Why do we groom horses and ponies?

2. When you are using a brush, do you follow the direction in which the coat grows or work against it?

3. What do you use a water brush for?

4. What do you use a stable cloth for?

5. In cold weather, how can you keep a clipped pony warm while you groom it?

6. What do you use to remove dried mud?

7. How do you brush out a tail?

8. What kind of brush should you use on a pony's face?

9. What is a hoof pick for?

10. What do you do with damp sponges?

11. Name the items of the grooming kit shown below.

a)

b)

c)

d)

e)

f)

g)

h)

29

Feeding Time

1. What is a pony's natural food?

   Grass

2. What do we replace this natural food with when we keep ponies in stables?

   use hay

3. What is meant by "hard feed?" Pellets

4. Should you give a pony a different kind of food at each meal?

   NO

5. What must you do with sugar beet before you feed it to a pony? IDK

6. What is chaff? What is it used for?

7. Is it better to feed two large meals or several small ones in a day? 2 large feeds

8. Why might you feed soaked hay to a pony?

   IDK

9. What kind of pony food looks like your breakfast cereal?

10. How can you provide a pony with salt and minerals?

Hay Barn

There are lots of hay nets in this picture. Which two are identical?

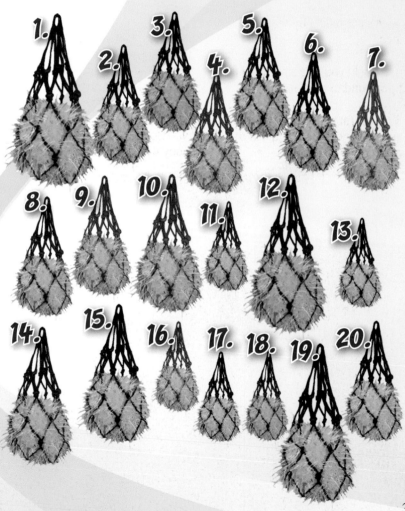

Bridle-wise

Do you know your way around a double bridle? See if you can name all the numbered parts.

Picture Negative

Here's a picture of a piebald pony, and below it are several negative images of the picture. Only one of them matches it exactly. Can you spot which one it is?

Horsy Words

Do you know the meanings of these horsy words? You have a one in three chance of getting each one right.

1. Leading file means ...
a) The first file a farrier uses on a pony's foot
b) The leading horse and rider in a group
c) A metal trim on a stable door to stop a pony chewing it

2. Flat work means ...
a) Schooling a pony on the ground, not over fences
b) Cleaning out a stable
c) Design inscribed on a Western saddle

3. A bounce fence is ...
a) An upright fence
b) A double fence in which the second part is higher than the first
c) A double fence without a stride between the two elements

4. A transition is ...
a) A change from one pace to another
b) A horse or pony that has one Thoroughbred parent
c) A partition that divides two looseboxes

5. "Pointing" means ...
a) The black lower legs, mane and tail of a bay horse
b) Rasping a horse's or pony's teeth
c) A horse or pony standing with one foreleg stuck out markedly in front of the other. It usually shows that the foot on that leg is painful.

6. An eel stripe is ...
a) A white mark down the pony's nose
b) A dark mark along the pony's spine
c) A dark mark on the pony's hock

7. Feather is ...
a) Long hair that grows on the lower legs of some horses and ponies
b) Long hair that grows under some horses' and ponies' jaws
c) A very thick and long mane and forelock

8. A manege is ...
a) Part of a driving harness that carries the reins
b) An enclosed arena for riding and schooling
c) A split in the front of a horse's or pony's hoof

Riding Out and Road Safety

You're going out for a trail ride – but do you know the rules for riding on the road? It's important that you do, so check just how much you know.

1. What should you always do before you set out on a trail ride on your own?

2. When you ride out on a road, should you be on the same side as the traffic?

3. What should you do if you want to turn left and there is a car behind you?

4. If a rider raises her arm straight up in traffic, what does that signal mean?

5. Is it safe to canter along the side of the road?

6. Is it safe to ride two or more horses side-by-side on a road?

7. What should you do if a vehicle is approaching at a high speed and you know your pony is nervous?

8. What should you do if a vehicle slows down and passes you carefully, allowing lots of room?

9. If you ride past a field of cows or other horses, what must you be aware of?

10. Why might you wear one of these?

11. What should you make sure of before crossing a stream?

12. If you are riding side-by-side, which rider should give the hand signal for turning right or left?

PLEASE PASS
WIDE & SLOW

HORSEWARE

On the Hoof

An old saying goes, "No foot, no horse!" which shows how important the state of a pony's hooves is to its health. See how much you know about ponies' feet with these questions.

1. What does the outer casing of a pony's foot consist of?

2. What is the inner part of a pony's foot made up of?

3. What should you do with a pony's feet every day?

4. How do you pick up a pony's front foot?

5. What is the function of the frog?

6. How often do a pony's feet need trimming?

7. Why do ponies wear shoes?

8. If a pony has a white sock, what color will the foot be on that leg?

9. Is hoof oil good for a pony's feet?

10. What happens if the hooves become overgrown?

Parts of the Hoof

Can you name the numbered parts of the hoof?

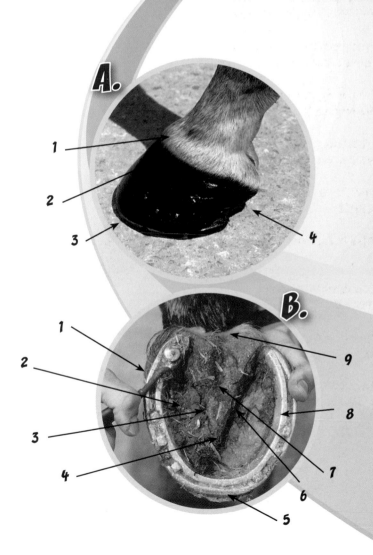

Jumping Ring

Do you know what these show jumps are called?

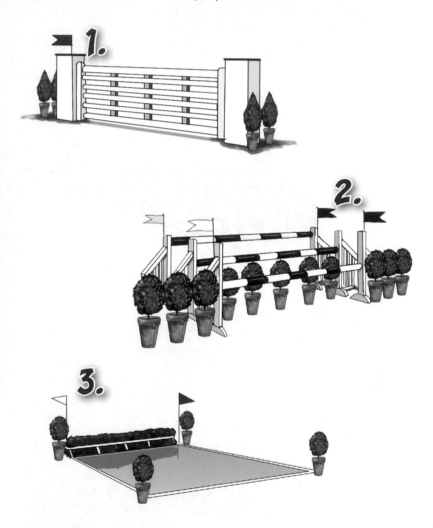

1.

2.

3.

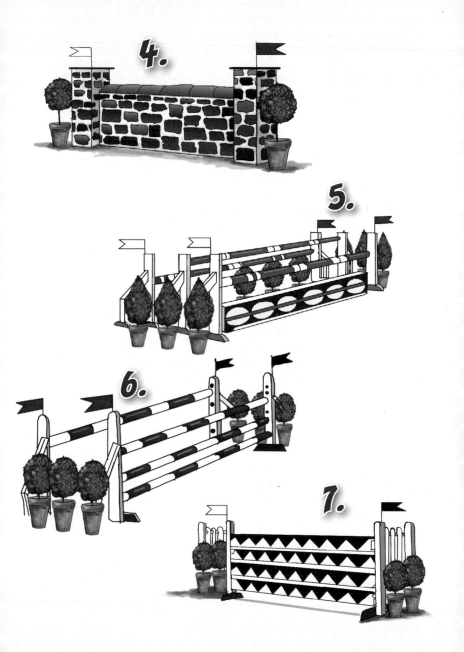

Where?

1. Where on a horse or pony would you find the cannon bone?

2. Where does the breed of horse called the Waler come from?

3. Where is the Luhmuhlen three-day event held?

4. Where is the head-quarters of the Spanish Riding School?

5. Where would you fit a crupper?

6. Where would you use a sweat scraper?

7. Where on a horse or pony is the ergot?

8. Where does the Akhal-Teke horse come from?

9. Where would you put a kimblewick?

10. Where, on a harness horse, would you find hames?

What Connects?

The words in each of these groups all have something in common. Do you know what it is?

1. Bandages, brushing boots, over-reach boots.
2. Half-pass, shoulder-in, full pass.
3. Hunter, blanket, trace.
4. Hunter, cob, show.
5. Coarse mix, flaked corn, chaff.
6. Pritchel, rasp, drawing knife.
7. Roller, surcingle, girth.
8. Red worms, bots, lice.
9. Spanish walk, piaffe, levade.
10. Hackney, Standardbred, American Shetland.

Keeping a Pony Healthy

If you have a pony of your own you should be able to answer all these questions.

1. How often does a horse or pony need worming?

2. What should a healthy pony's temperature be when it is resting?

3. Where on the pony's head can you feel its pulse?

4. If a pony is lame in a foreleg, it nods its head when it is walked or trotted out. Does it do this when the lame leg hits the ground, or as its good leg hits the ground?

5. Should a pony's feet feel hot or cool?

6. Should a pony's legs feel hot or cool?

7. What diseases are horses and ponies commonly vaccinated against?

8. What do ponies do if they have sweet itch?

Treating a Sick Pony

Sometimes, no matter how hard you try, a pony can get sick. Would you know how to care for it?

1. Why might a pony be standing with his foot in a bucket?

2. Sometimes a pony can get little yellow specks on its leg. Why might they be harmful?

3. If a pony looks distressed, is sweating, and keeps lying down and getting up again, and possibly rolling, what is most likely wrong with it?

4. What is most likely wrong with this horse, below?

What on Earth?

These weird-looking objects are all ordinary things from the horsy world, but they have been photographed from odd angles. How many of them can you recognize?

1. styurp

2. helmet

3. Spur

4. hOOF cover

Leg cover

5.

Brush

6.

Reins

7.

bit

8.

47

What a Load of Nonsense!

This paragraph contains a lot of very silly deliberate mistakes. How many can you spot?

Jenny was looking forward to her ride. She was going to take out her friend Jamie's four-year-old gray thoroughpin fillet Snowball for a trail ride along the lanes and through the woods. Snowball was only 12.2 hands high, but Jenny wasn't very tall, so she fit her quite well. When Jenny arrived at the stables, she found Snowball already saddled. He was a tall horse, so she led him to the mountain block so she could get on more easily. Once up on his broad chestnut back, she headed out of the yard and down the lane, heading for the beach. She gave the pony a gallop, and when she had pulled her up, decided to try a little dressing. She trotted a circle to the right, then changed the rain and cantered a figure-nine, doing a floating change in the center. Then she stopped

Snowstorm, and did a turn on the forehead. The large old bay horse be-haved very well, and Jenny was pleased with him. She gave him a pat on his shiny black neck, and trotted back along the lane, heading for home. When she got back, she would give him his feed – a bowl of bread and milk – before putting him out in the paddock, where he could enjoy himself watching television with his friends.

Making Tracks

Look carefully at each pony's feet and see if you can trace the hoofprints each one left on its route through the woods.

1.

2.

3.

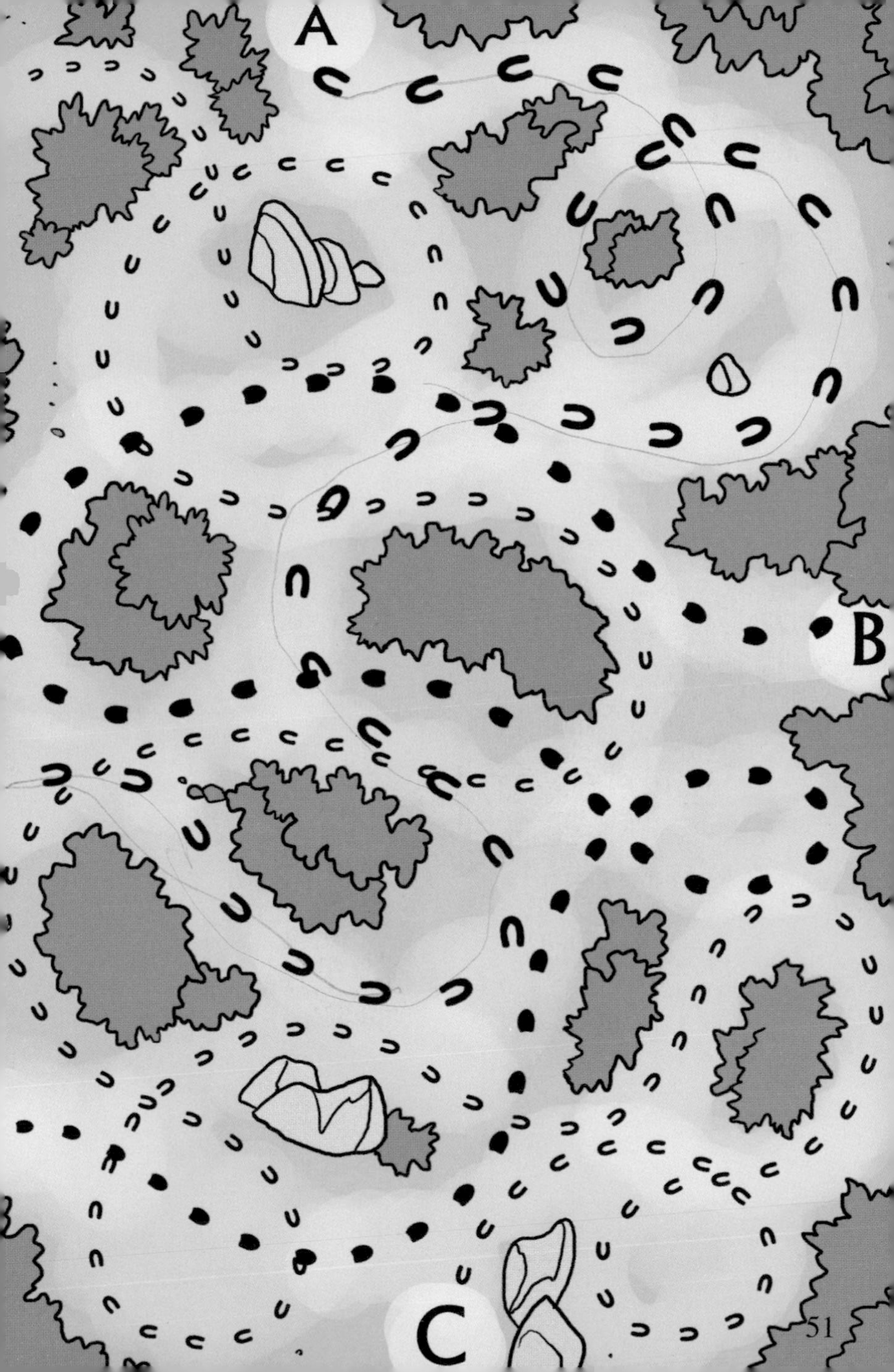
A
B
C

Horse Body Language

Horses and ponies can communicate with us and with each other by the ways in which they move their bodies, the expressions on their faces, and their general behavior. This kind of communication is called body language. Take a look at these pictures and see if you can tell what each one is "saying."

1.

2.

3.

4.

5.

6.

7.

8.

Eventing

1. What sections does a three-day event consist of?

2. Do one- and two-day events have the same sections?

3. How are the jumping sections scored?

4. How does a horse have to act in order to succeed in eventing?

5. Who was World Champion in eventing in 2006?

6. Why might a rider put studs in their horse's shoes?

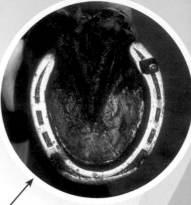

7. When a rider completes their dressage test, what do they do before leaving the arena?

8. Is the jumping in eventing against the clock?

9. What does CCI stand for?

Over the Fences

How many of these cross-country fences can you name?

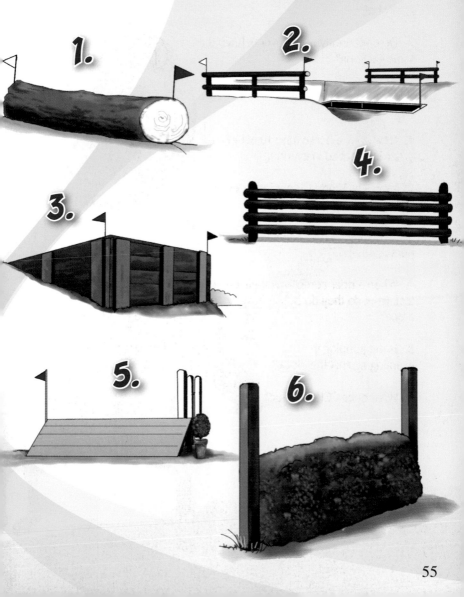

Getting Ready for a Ride

Sally is getting her pony Bramble ready to go out for a ride. The pictures show some of the things she does to prepare for her ride, but they have been put in the wrong order. Can you put them in the correct order?

1.

2.

3.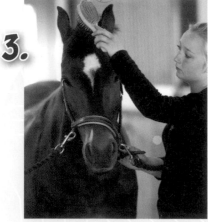

4.

5.

6.

7.

8.

9.

10.

11.

12.

True or False?

Which of the following statements are true and which are false?

1. A steeplechase is a race over fences.

2. Walking is a four-beat pace.

3. When you ride, the palms of your hands should face downwards.

4. Stirrups on Western saddles are made of wood.

5. Brushing boots are what a horse or pony wears when it is traveling in a horsebox or trailer.

6. When riding in the cross-country phase of an event, you jump a fence with the red flag on the right and the white on the left.

7. A wisp is made of hay or straw and used to massage the neck, shoulder, quarters and thigh muscles of a horse or pony after hard work.

8. Bran mash is very nourishing.

9. In winter, more of the food a horse or pony eats is used to keep it warm.

10. It is important for a pony's health that its stable is well ventilated.

In the Saddle

Do you know how to sit correctly on a pony?

1. When you are sitting in the saddle, should your legs be bent at the knees or straight?

2. Which part of your foot should rest in the stirrup iron?

3. When you are sitting correctly, a vertical line should pass through certain parts of your body. Which are they?

4. If you let your leg hang down naturally beside the stirrup, and, if the stirrup is the correct length, where would the tread of the iron be in relation to your foot?

5. Which of these riders is holding the reins correctly?

6. How can you tighten the girth when sitting in the saddle?

7. There should be a straight line from the pony's bit along the reins to your elbow. True or false?

Foals in the Field

All these foals look very similar, but only two of them are identical. Can you spot which two they are?

Horses in History

See how much you know about the history of the horse.

1. The earliest horses lived around 55 million years ago. True or false?

2. Was this earliest horse larger or smaller than present-day horses?

3. When did people first start to drive horses? Was it around 3,500 BC, around 1,000 BC or around AD 500?

4. Were horses first raced harnessed to chariots or being ridden?

5. Knights in armor rode horses into battle. What kind of horses did they ride? Were they:
a) Light, fast horses like Thoroughbreds?
b) Large, heavy horses like cart horses or draught horses?
c) Stocky ponies like Highlands or Haflingers?

6. How did women ride from the 14th to the early 20th century?

7. When were stirrups first used in Europe? Was it 1,500 years ago, 1,000 years ago or 500 years ago?

8. How did Federico Caprilli revolutionize jumping?

Points of the Horse

The visible parts of a horse's or pony's anatomy are called the "points of a horse." How many of the numbered points can you name?

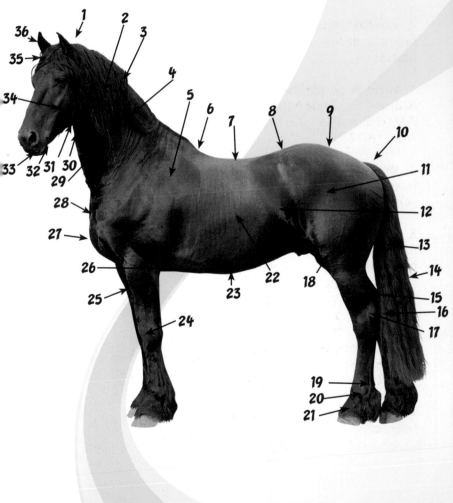

Horse and Pony Breeds

How much do you know about the many different breeds of horses and ponies?

1. What is the fastest breed of horse in the world?

2. Which breed of pony comes from western Ireland and is often a good jumper?

3. Which British breed of horse and pony is a very high-stepping harness animal?

4. Which hugely muscled heavy horse is believed to be the most massively built of all the European draft horses?

5. Where do the Konik and Hucul ponies come from?

6. Which South American breed is considered to be the toughest and soundest breed in the world, and is often crossed with Thoroughbreds to produce polo ponies?

7. Which ancient and beautiful breed of horse from the Middle East has had a great influence on horse and pony breeding throughout the world?

8. Which American breed of horse was named after a man?

9. Which breed from southern Spain is descended from the ancient Spanish Horse and is used for dressage and in harness?

Find a Route

It's not the sort of field you should keep a pony in, but can you choose the correct route across it to the stable yard avoiding streams, boggy patches, bushes, ragwort and other hazards?

Riding in the Ring

You're having a lesson with some other riders in the ring. See how much you know about what goes on.

1. Are these riders the correct distance apart?

2. You might be asked to do exercises such as touching your toes or lying back on the pony's back while you are in the saddle. What is the purpose of them?

3. You might also ride without reins or without stirrups. Why?

4. If you are told to walk to letter B and then trot, at which point should you break into a trot? Is it as the pony's nose reaches the letter, as its shoulder reaches the letter, or as its rider reaches the letter?

5. You might ride along a shape like this. What is it called?

6. And what are these shapes called?

a)

b)

7. If you ride alongside another pony as a pair, which pony has to go faster when you go around a corner – the pony on the inside or the pony on the outside?

8. Why might you be on a leading rein or a lungeing rein for your first few riding lessons?

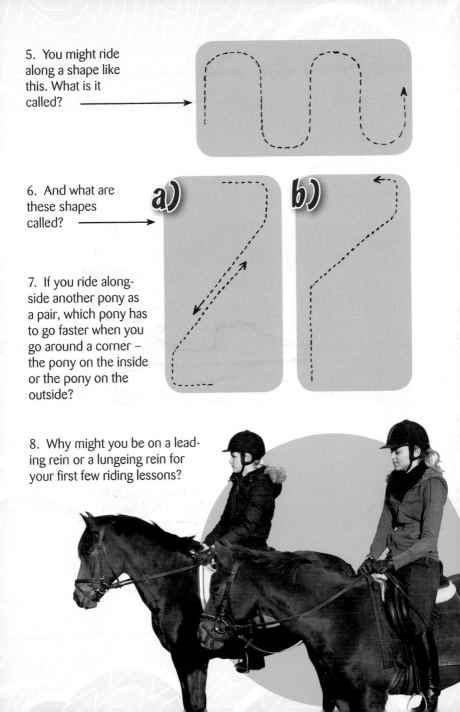

Odd One Out

Can you spot the odd one out in each of these lists of words?

1. Skewbald, bay, piebald.

2. Blaze, sock, stocking.

3. Walk, gallop, trot. (This is a sneaky one!)

4. Cantle, cheekpiece, headpiece.

5. Loose-ring, half-moon, eggbutt.

6. Wall, incisor, white line.

7. Colic, ringbone, navicular disease.

8. Dandelions, buttercups, nettles.

9. Chaff, haylage, oats.

10. Hawthorn, yew, laurel.

Ponies Galore!

Anna, Belinda and Celia are lucky children, since they each have several ponies. They all keep their ponies in this field, together with those belonging to other people. If all of Anna's ponies are chestnut, with three white socks and a white blaze, and all of Belinda's ponies are bay, with no white socks and a white star, and all of Celia's ponies are skewbald with black manes and tails, how many ponies do Anna, Belinda and Celia have in the field?

A Mixed Bag

You have a mostly one in three chance of getting the answers correct in this quiz. (One question has two correct answers!)

1. Where should the light switches be in a stable?
a) Outside
b) Just inside the door at hand height
c) Inside the door at floor level

2. Why is it not a good idea to wear sandals when handling ponies and cleaning out stables?
a) Because your feet will get dirty
b) Because the pony could step on your feet and hurt you
c) Because you might injure your feet with pitchforks, shovels, wheelbarrows, etc.

3. Who, in ancient Greece, wrote a book about horsemanship whose principles are still in use today? Was it ...
a) Socrates
b) Plato
c) Xenophon

4. If a pony kicks forwards with a hind leg, what is it called?
a) Donkey kicking
b) Cow kicking
c) Fly kicking

5. You can check the approximate length of your stirrup leathers before you mount a pony by measuring them along your arm. Where do you measure them?
a) From fingertips to armpit
b) From fingertips to elbow
c) From wrist to armpit

Mirror Image

The four lower pictures are mirror images of the top picture, but only one of them is the exact mirror image. Can you spot which one it is?

1.

2.

3.

4.

Horses in History and Mythology

1. What was the name of Bellerophon's winged horse of Greek mythology?

2. Whose horse was made a Roman senator, and what was its name?

3. What did Diomedes' mares eat?

4. What was Napoleon's favorite horse named? He was ridden at the battle of Waterloo and appears in a famous painting.

5. The Duke of Wellington's horse, which carried him at Waterloo, was named after another battle and, when he died 21 years later, was buried with full military honors. What was his name?

6. What was Don Quixote's thin horse called?

7. Alexander the Great's famous horse lived to the age of 30. What was his name?

8. Bayard was given by King Charlemagne to the four sons of Aymon. What was extraordinary about him?

9. Who ordered the making of the wooden horse of Troy?

10. What were the half-man, half-horse creatures of ancient Greece called?

11. How, according to legend, could a unicorn be caught?

What Are These?

Do you know what all these pieces of horse equipment are called?

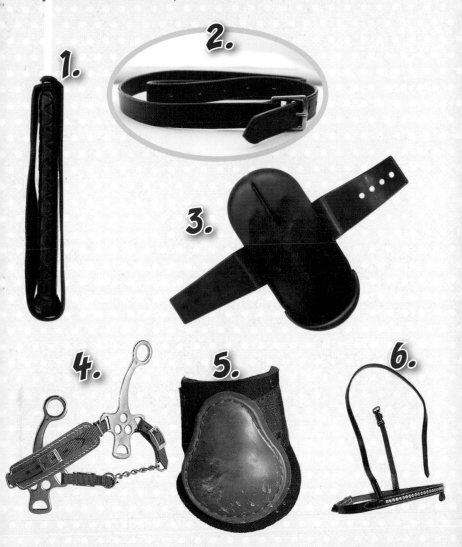

1.

2.

3.

4.

5.

6.

Spot the Differences

These kids are busy getting the ponies at the riding school ready for their day's work. The two pictures may look exactly the same, but there are several differences between them. How many can you spot?

Baffling Brainteasers

These puzzles will really test your mental powers!

1. A number of ponies and their riders set off on a trail ride. There were two ponies and their riders in front of a pony and its rider, two ponies and their riders behind a pony and its rider, and a pony and its rider in the middle. How many ponies (and their riders) were there altogether?

2. Judy collected 33 carrots from a box in the pantry and carried them in four bags to the stables to give to the ponies. Each bag contained an odd number of carrots. How was this possible? (It is possible – think about it!)

3. A bridle and a bit cost $120. The bridle cost $100 more than the bit. What was the price of each?

4. Carrie owned a number of Shetland ponies. All but two of them were gray, all but two of them were bay, all but two of them were chestnut. How many Shetland ponies did Carrie have?

5. Annie, Brian, Carol, David and Edie were the only entrants in the under-sixteen jumping class at the local show. David did not come in first. Annie came in before Brian. Carol came in last. Only three of them were placed in alphabetical order. Who won the class, and what positions did the others get?

All Squared Up

In this picture of a rider jumping in the show ring, two of the squares are exactly the same. Can you spot which two they are?

How?

1. How do you take a horse's or pony's temperature?

2. How can you give a visible warning to other riders that your pony is liable to kick others?

3. How can you tell a horse's or pony's age?

4. How should you lead a pony on the road if you are riding another pony?

5. How do you worm a horse or pony?

6. How should you feed hay to a horse or pony?

7. How should you tie up a horse or pony?

8. How should you use a hoof pick?

9. How can you safely open a pony's mouth?

10. How do you fasten a braid in a pony's mane?

Moving Forward

Can you tell from the drawings at what paces each of these ponies is moving?

1.

2.

3.

4.

5.

Observation Test

How good are your powers of observation? Study the picture on the right for one minute (time yourself with a watch), then cover the picture with a sheet of paper, turn the book upside down and see if you can answer the questions below.

1. What color hair does the girl jumping the chestnut pony over a practice fence have?
2. What color is her hat?
3. Is the bay pony with the girl in the red shirt wearing a saddle?
4. How many people are lined up for ice-cream?
5. Who is walking a small white dog?
6. Where is the boy grazing a Shetland pony?
7. What is on the side of the horse trailer?
8. What is happening to the piebald pony?

Answers

Page 8 Ponies! Ponies! Ponies!
Front row: Silver, Bella
Back row: Snowball, Biscuit, Jess, Rhoda, Jewel and Daisy

Page 10 Make and Shape
1. The shoulders and pasterns.

2. A neck that is concave in profile on its top line, like that of a sheep.

3. A face that is concave in profile. The Arab is famous for it.

4. It refers to the measurement around the cannon bone just below the knee.

5. Cow hocks.

6. The front legs.

7. Ears that flop forwards or to the side.

8. Just above the hoof.

9. Pigeon toes.

10. A broad chest.

11. Hindquarters that slope steeply down from the croup to the dock.

12. A roach back. (Too straight.)

13. Flat.

14. Its hindquarters.

Page 12 Why?

1. In case the pony panics and pulls backwards. The string would break and this could prevent the pony from injuring itself.

2. If leather is neglected it can dry out and break, which could be dangerous. If it is kept clean and supple it does not. Cleaning the tack also allows the opportunity to check it over.

3. For neatness, to show the shape of the neck and to help make the neck look a good shape.

4. They do not slip in wet weather.

5. To keep it from getting strewn on the ground and wasted. The hay bag must be at the right height – not too high, as horses do not like to stretch their necks upwards for food, and dust and seeds can fall into their eyes; nor too low or the horse risks catching a foot in the net.

6. The tradition dates back to the days when riders carried swords on their left sides and therefore had to mount their horses from the left side.

7. Because unless they have plenty of fresh air, horses and ponies can suffer from respiratory problems.

8. To keep the curb chain in the chin groove.

Page 13 Name the Markings

1. White coronet stripe.   2. White heel.   3. Zebra marks on hock.
4. White sock.   5. White stocking.   6. White pastern.   7. White coronet.

Page 14 Mounting and Dismounting

1. Turn the back of the iron toward you.

2. The left foot.

3. Stand it facing a wall or gate.

4. Kick the pony with your foot.

5. No.

6. A leg up.

7. A mounting block on which you stand to make it easier to mount. This keeps you from pulling the saddle over as you mount, which is better for the horse's back, and it is easier on your muscles too.

8. Swap them over from time to time, otherwise the one on the mounting side will stretch and end up longer than the other.

9. Take both feet out of the stirrups.

10. The left hand.

11. Lean forwards.

12. For beginners: leave the reins on the horse's neck and hold them in your right hand, between the thumb and index finger, near the horse's head. For more experienced riders: bring the reins over the horse's head and hold them in your right hand, between the thumb and index finger, close to the horse's head. Hold the end of the reins in your left hand.

Page 16 Baffling Brainteasers
1. Four fillies and three colts.

2. Mrs. Black, taking three hours and just under seventeen minutes. Mrs. Brown took three hours and 42 minutes.

3. Twenty.

4. Forty.

5. Four.

Page 17 Odd One Out
Picture #3.

Page 18 Walk On
1. b). 2. a). 3. a). 4. c). 5. a). 6. a). 7. c).

Page 20 Saddling Up
1. No.

2. Just behind them.

3. Usually from the left, though it can be from the right. But because the horse is a creature of habit it is best to always do it from the same side.

4. They prevent the girth buckles from damaging the saddle flaps.

5. Fasten the girth one hole at a time, and check after each hole that the skin is smoothed out under the girth.

6. A numnah.

7. By loops on the girth straps and loops through which the girth slots.

8. On a saddle horse – either a bracket type or free-standing.

9. A tree.

10. Three. There must be a space all the way along the "saddle tunnel" between the numnah and the horse's back.

Page 21 Parts of the Saddle
1. Pommel.   2. Seat.   3. Cantle.   4. Panel.   5. Saddle flap.
6. Stirrup leather.   7. Stirrup.   8. Girth.   9. Knee Roll.

Page 22 True or False?
1. True.

2. False, they are gold-colored with white manes and tails.

3. False, it is a place where horses and ponies are kept.

4. False, the heel should be down and the toe up.

5. True.

6. False, it is the same as with brown eyes.

7. True.

8. True.

9. False, it's a mane comb.

10. False, it makes it unmanageable.

11. True.

12. True.

13. True.

14. False, it's a change of leading leg at the canter "in the air."

Page 24 What's Wrong?
Here are the deliberate mistakes:

1. One box has the top door closed and the lower door open.

2. One box has a pony with its head over the door eating the flowers in a hanging basket.

3. The muck heap is in the middle of the yard.

4. A mounting block is lying on its side.

5. A saddle is lying in the yard.

6. A girl is leading a pony with bare feet.

7. A rider is sitting on a pony. She is not wearing a helmet, the saddle has no stirrups, the pony has only three legs, the rein is attached wrong.

8. A horse trailer is hitched to a bicycle.

9. Water from a tap is running into a bucket but it has been left so the bucket is overflowing – that's a lot of water running out.

10. The door of the feed room is open, lids are off the feed bins and rats are running around.

11. A jump is set up in the yard.

12. Someone is clipping a dog with horse clippers.

Page 26 A Pony's Paces

1. Walk, trot, canter and gallop.

2. In diagonal pairs.

3. Both legs on the same side move together.

4. Yes.

5. Gallop.

6. A fast, running walk.

7. Icelandic.

8. Three.

9. In the collected canter the strides are shorter, so the pony covers less ground and its speed is decreased.

10. They are lowered.

Page 27 Galloping Ponies

There are 8 ponies galloping to the left and 6 ponies galloping to the right.

Page 28 Good Grooming

1. To keep them clean and to increase the blood circulation.

2. Follow the direction in which the coat grows.

3. Laying the hair of the mane and tail flat.

4. Giving a final "polish" by removing any dust and loose hairs.

5. By folding its rug over the part you are not grooming, i.e. the shoulders or hindquarters.

6. A dandy brush, and rubber and plastic curry combs.

7. By holding the tail in one hand and with the other hand taking small sections, one at a time, and combing downwards. You can also separate tangled hairs in the tail with your fingers.

8. A soft one such as a body brush.

9. Removing dirt and stones from the feet.

10. Clean around the eyes, nose and dock.

11. a) Dandy brush.   b) Body brush.   c) Metal curry comb.
d) Rubber curry comb.   e) Plastic curry comb.   f) Mane comb.
g) Hoof pick.   h) Sponge.

Page 30   Feeding Time

1. Grass.

2. Hay or haylage.

3. Concentrates such as oats plus coarse mixes, pony nuts and so on.

4. No.

5. Soak it in water for at least an hour.

6. Chopped hay and straw. It is mixed with hard feed to help slow down the pony's eating by giving it more to chew on and thus helping its digestion.

7. Several small meals.

8. If you soak the hay in a big bucket or tub for a while the dust will be washed out into the water. This helps ponies with breathing problems.

9. Flaked corn.

10. With a mineral lick.

Page 31   Hay Barn
Hay nets 2 and 5 are identical.

Page 32   Bridlewise
1. Headpiece.
2. Browband.
3. Throatlash.
4. Bridoon cheekpiece.
5. Weymouth cheekpiece.
6. Noseband.
7. Weymouth bit.
8. Bridoon bit.
9. Curb chain.
10. Lip strap.
11. Curb rein.
12. Bridoon (snaffle) rein.

Page 33   Picture Negative
Image number 4 matches the picture exactly.

Page 34   Horsy Words
1. b).   2. a).   3. c).   4. a).   5. c).   6. b).   7. a).   8. b).

Page 36 Riding Out and Road Safety

1. Tell an adult where you are going and when you expect to be back. Carry a cell phone if you can, and wear a yellow reflective vest, even in the daytime (see question 10). For your safety, it is always best to have company when riding out.

2. Yes.

3. Look behind you. If the car is close or traveling fast, pull off and wait until it has passed. Otherwise give the hand signal for turning left in plenty of time and move over to the left.

4. Stop.

5. No, not on a road.

6. It depends on the road and the horses or ponies. Generally it is safer to ride in single file. Side-by-side may be safe if the road is wide enough and not too fast, and an inexperienced pony can be kept on the inside of a more experienced one and away from the traffic. More than two is not safe.

7. If possible, ride on to the side of the road and stop. Ask the vehicle to slow down by waving your arm slowly up and down.

8. Smile and thank them by waving your hand or nodding your head.

9. They may charge up to you and upset your pony.

10. It's a safety vest that reflects the light and helps you to be more visible on the road.

11. Check to make sure the water is not too deep and that there is firm footing.

12. The rider on the inside of the turn.

Page 38   On the Hoof

1. Horn, composed of insensitive leaves, or laminae.

2. Bones encased in sensitive fleshy laminae.

3. Pick them out and check the shoes.

4. Slide your hand down the back of the leg to the fetlock, then move it around to the front of the leg and lift.

5. It acts as a shock absorber.

6. Every six to eight weeks.

7. To keep their feet from wearing down too quickly and becoming sore.

8. Usually white, i.e. light-colored, but there are exceptions.

9. No, but it makes them look good.

10. The weight goes back on the pony's heels which alters the foot's balance. It takes a long time to correct.

Page 39   Parts of the Hoof

A: 1. Coronet.   2. Wall of foot.   3. Heel.   4. Toe.
B: 1. Wall of foot.   2. Sole.   3. Frog.   4. Point of frog.   5. Toe.
6. Bars of foot.   7. Cleft of frog.   8. White line.   9. Heel.

Page 40 Jumping Ring
1. Gate. 2. Triple bar. 3. Water. 4. Wall. 5. Hog's back.
6. Double oxer. 7. Planks.

Page 42 Where?
1. Between the knee and fetlock joints.

2. Australia.

3. Germany.

4. Vienna.

5. On the back of the saddle to and around the top of the tail.

6. On a pony's coat, to remove excess sweat, or water when washing.

7. At the back of the fetlock joint.

8. Turkmenistan, north of Iran.

9. In a pony's mouth – it's a bit.

10. On the collar of the harness.

Page 43 What Connects?
1. They all protect a horse's or pony's lower legs.

2. They are all lateral movements, or "work on two tracks."

3. They are all types of clipping.

4. They are all types of riding horse.

5. They are all types of feed.

6. They are all farrier's tools.

7. They all go around a horse's or pony's middle to hold rugs/saddle on.

8. They are all parasites of horses and ponies.

9. They are all dressage movements.

10. They are all breeds of driving horses/ponies.

Page 44   Keeping a Pony Healthy

1. It depends on the type of wormer, but usually every six to twelve weeks. Ask your vet what is best for your horse. Young horses need worming more often; an adult horse may only need worming four to five times a year. They always need worming before and after periods out at pasture.

2. 99.5 degrees fahrenheit to 101.3 degrees fahrenheit.

3. Under the jawbone.

4. As the good leg hits the ground.

5. Cool.

6. Cool.

7. Equine flu and tetanus.

8. Rub their manes and tails.

Page 45 Treating a Sick Pony

1. It's called tubbing. The pony stands with its foot in a bucket of warm water and Epsom salts which helps draw infection out of the hoof.

2. They are bots – eggs which the pony licks off and which then give it internal parasites.

3. Colic.

4. Laminitis. (It's leaning back, trying to put the weight on its heels.)

Page 46 What on Earth?

1. A stirrup iron.

2. A riding hat.

3. A spur.

4. A riding boot.

5. A rubber boot.

6. A brush.

7. A rein.

8. A bit.

Page 48 What a Load of Nonsense!

1. Thoroughpin should be Thoroughbred.

2. Fillet should be filly.

3. A Thoroughbred wouldn't be 12.2 hands high. That's too short.

4. "He was a tall horse" – he's changed sex and height.

5. Mountain block should be mounting block.

6. "Broad chestnut back" – a Thoroughbred wouldn't be broad, and he/she started out as a gray.

7. "She gave the pony a gallop" – it's back to being a pony and it's changed sex again.

8. Dressing should be dressage.

9. Rain should be rein.

10. Figure-nine should be figure-eight.

11. Floating change should be flying change.

12. Snowball has become Snowstorm.

13. Turn on the forehead should be turn on the forehand.

14. The horse has now become a large bay and changed sex again.

15. He's now become black.

16. You don't feed horses bread and milk.

17. And they don't watch television in the paddock with their friends!

Page 50   Making Tracks
Pony 1 track A.
Pony 2 track C.
Pony 3 track B.

Page 52 Horse Body Language

1. "I'm mad" or, "I'm listening to something behind me."

2. "That looks interesting."

3. "I'm trying to concentrate on two things at once."

4. "I'm very angry."

5. "I'm very angry and I might bite you."

6. "I'm miserable and cold and not feeling well."

7. "Hurry up! I'm fed up with waiting and want to get on with things."

8. "If you come closer I'll kick you."

Page 54 Eventing

1. Dressage, cross-country and show jumping.

2. Yes.

3. By penalty points.

4. It must be well schooled and obedient for its rider to carry out dressage, fast and bold to gallop and jump cross-country, and a careful show jumper.

5. Zara Phillips (granddaughter of Queen Elizabeth II of England).

6. To keep it from slipping in mud.

7. They bow to the judges.

8. No, but there is a time allowance. If you exceed it you get penalty points.

9. Concours Complet International.

Page 55 Over the Fences
1. Log.   2. Coffin.   3. Bank.   4. Rails.   5. Ski jump.   6. Hedge.

Page 56 Getting Ready for a Ride
Picture #5 should be 1.

Picture #2 is correct.

Picture #9 should be 3.

Picture #6 should be 4.

Picture #3 should be 5.

Picture #12 should be 6.

Picture #11 should be 7.

Picture #1 should be 8.

Picture #7 should be 9.

Picture #4 should be 10.

Picture #8 should be 11.

Picture #10 should be 12.

Page 59 True or False?
1. True.

2. True.

3. False, they should face each other, and be almost closed. You should hold the reins as if you are gently holding a small bird in your hands.

4. True, on traditional saddles.

5. False, they protect the horse's lower legs when being ridden.

6. True.

7. True.

8. False.

9. True.

10. True.

Page 60   In the Saddle

1. Bent at the knees.

2. The ball of your foot.

3. Ear, shoulder, hip, heel.

4. Level with your instep.

5. Rider 1.

6. Put your leg in front of the saddle flap, lift the flap and pull each girth strap up separately.

7. True.

Page 61 Foals in the Field
Foals #1 and #4 are identical.

Page 62 Horses in History
1. True.

2. Smaller.

3. Around 3,500 BC.

4. Harnessed to chariots.

5. b).

6. Sidesaddle.

7. 1,500 years ago.

8. He invented the forward seat.

Page 63 Points of the Horse
1. Poll.
2. Neck.
3. Crest.
4. Mane.
5. Shoulder.
6. Withers.
7. Back.
8. Loins.
9. Croup.
10. Dock.
11. Point of hip.
12. Flank.
13. Thigh.

14. Tail.
15. Gaskin.
16. Point of hock.
17. Hock.
18. Stifle.
19. Fetlock joint.
20. Pastern.
21. Coronary band.
22. Ribs.
23. Belly.
24. Knee.
25. Forearm.
26. Elbow.
27. Chest.
28. Point of shoulder.
29. Jugular groove.
30. Throat.
31. Cheek.
32. Chin groove.
33. Muzzle.
34. Cheekbone.
35. Forelock.
36. Ear.

Page 64 Horse and Pony Breeds
1. Thoroughbred.
2. Connemara.
3. Hackney Horse/Pony.
4. Dutch Draft.
5. Poland/Romania.
6. Criollo.
7. Arab.
8. Morgan.
9. Andalusian.

Page 65 Find a Route
(See drawing below.)

Page 66 Riding in the Ring
1. Yes.

2. To keep you supple and help build up your confidence.

3. To improve your balance and stop you from relying on stirrups and reins to maintain your balance.

4. As the pony's shoulder reaches the letter.

5. Serpentines.

6. a) Diagonal.   b) Short diagonal.

7. The pony on the outside.

8. So you can concentrate on your seat in the saddle and give the aids without having to control the pony.

Page 68 Odd One Out
1. Bay; the others are not solid colors.

2. Blaze; it is a face marking, the others are leg markings.

3. Trot; it is a two-beat pace, the others are four-beat paces.

4. Cantle; it is part of a saddle,

the others are parts of a bridle.

5. Half-moon; it is a type of pelham bit, the others are types of snaffle bit.

6. Incisor; it is a tooth, the others are parts of the foot.

7. Colic; it is a disorder of the intestines, the others are foot problems.

8. Buttercup; it is a harmful plant, the others are nutritious.

9. Oats; they are a hard feed, the others are fodder feeds.

10. Hawthorn; it is edible, the others are poisonous.

Page 69   Ponies Galore!
Anna has 3 ponies. Belinda has 3 ponies. Celia has 2 ponies.

Page 70   A Mixed Bag
1. a).   2. b) and c).   3. c).   4. b).   5. a).

Page 71   Mirror Image
Picture number 3 is the correct mirror image.

Page 72   Horses in History and Mythology
1. Pegasus.

2. Emperor Caligula's horse, Incitatus.

3. Human flesh.

4. Marengo.

5. Copenhagen.

6. Rocinante.

7. Bucephalus.

8. He could elongate his body so all four could ride at once.

9. Odysseus (or Ulysses).

10. Centaurs.

11. It could not be caught by a man but would voluntarily lay its head in a maiden's lap.

Page 73 What Are These?
1. Handle of a whip.
2. Stirrup leather.
3. Plastic curry comb.
4. Hackamore.
5. Brush boot.
6. Noseband.

Page 74 Spot the Differences
There are 10 differences – see answer key on the opposite page.

Page 76 Baffling Brainteasers
1. Three.

2. Eleven in each of three bags and the three bags put in a fourth.

3. The bridle costs $110, the bit $10.

4. Three.

5. Edie first, David second, Annie third, Brian fourth, Carol fifth.

Page 77   All Squared Up
Squares B6 and D8 are identical.

Page 78 How?

1. By putting a greased thermometer in its anus.

2. Tie a red ribbon on its tail.

3. By its teeth and general appearance.

4. In a bridle, on the inside, so the ridden pony is nearest to the traffic.

5. By mixing worming powder in its feed or squirting worming paste onto its tongue from a special applicator.

6. In the stable, best in a hay net, though it can be fed on the floor. In the field, best at a "hay-table."

7. With a quick-release knot.

8. From heel to toe.

9. By putting your thumb in the corner of the mouth where there are no teeth.

10. With rubber bands or by sewing them in place.

Page 79 Moving Forwards

1. Canter. 2. Trot. 3. Gallop. 4. Gallop. 5. Walk.

Page 80 Observation Test

1. Blonde.

2. Blue.

3. No.

4. Four.

5. A man in a green shirt and tan trousers.

6. Behind the bushes.

7. A picture of a blue horse jumping.

8. It's being saddled.